The Berenstain Bears®
and the
GOOD DEED

Stan & Jan Berenstain

Reader's Digest **Kids**

Westport, Connecticut

It was going to be a big day for Bear Scouts Brother, Sister, and Cousin Fred. Today was the day they were going to get their Good Deed Merit Badges.

"Ready, Scouts?" said Scoutmaster Papa. "Let's go out and do a good deed."

"But first," said Brother, "we must find somebody to do a good deed for."

"That will be easy," said Papa. "There will be lots of bears who will need help today. I can feel it in my bones. Follow me, Scouts!"

So off they went to find
somebody to do a good deed for.

"Look!" said Papa. "Old Miz McGrizz is having trouble crossing the street! A perfect chance to do a good deed and get your merit badges."

"We're coming, Miz McGrizz!"
shouted Papa. "We will help
you cross the street!"

"Stop!" shouted Miz McGrizz. "I don't *want* to cross the street. I was waiting for a bus. Look! Now I've missed it!"

"Sorry about that," said Papa as Miz McGrizz chased them down the street.

"Do not worry, Scouts," said Papa. "We will find somebody to do a good deed for."

"Look!" he shouted. "Farmer Ben has fallen from his tractor, and the tractor is running away! A perfect chance to do a good deed and get your merit badges. Hurry! You go help Farmer Ben, and I'll stop the tractor."

But Farmer Ben didn't *need* help. "I didn't fall," he said. "I'm just resting."

Papa got a big log and threw it in
front of the runaway tractor.

But the tractor wasn't
running away. It was being
driven by Mrs. Ben.

"What do you think you're
doing, Papa Bear?" said Mrs.
Ben.

"Just trying to do a good
deed," said Papa.

"Humph!" said Mrs. Ben.

"Good deed, indeed!" said

Farmer Ben.

"Maybe we'd better go home
and try again tomorrow," said
Scout Sister.

"Nonsense!" said Scoutmaster
Papa. "A real Bear Scout never
quits! Besides, I know we're going
to find someone to do a good deed
for soon. I can feel it in my bones."

"Look! Up ahead!" Papa shouted. "Our friend Actual Factual is being attacked by bees! A perfect chance for you to get your merit badges.

"We're coming!" shouted
Papa. He took a bug bomb
from his pack. He sprayed
the bees that were attacking
Actual Factual.

But the bees were *not* attacking Actual Factual. They were *his* bees. He was their bee-keeper. Actual Factual did not get angry. Actual Factual never got angry. But the bees did. The bees got very angry.

They chased Papa. It's
a good thing he found a
pond to jump into or
those angry bees would
have stung him.

"Oh, dear," said Sister. "We will never get our merit badges."

"We will never find someone who needs help," said Brother.

"Every time we try to do a good deed we get into trouble," said Scout Fred.

"But not this time!" shouted Papa. "Look! Up there on that mountain on the edge of that cliff. That car is in trouble. I can feel it in my bones! Follow me!"

But when they got to the top of the mountain, the car was not in trouble.

"We're just enjoying the view," said the bears in the car.

The scouts looked at Papa. Papa looked at the scouts. "Well, you see," said Papa . . .

That's when Papa slipped and fell.

Down,
down,
down the
mountain he rolled,
onto the town
dump at the foot of
the mountain.

TOWN
DUMP

"I don't feel so good," said Papa. "My leg hurts. My arm hurts. I hurt all over. I can feel it in my bones."

"Papa is hurt," said Sister. "How will we ever get him home?"

"Look!" said Brother. He was pointing at an old wheelbarrow that somebody had thrown away. The scouts helped Papa into the wheelbarrow.

It wasn't easy. Papa was heavy.
But those three scouts pushed and
pulled, and pulled and pushed
until at last they got Papa home.

The scouts were sad.

"Why are you sad?" asked Mama Bear.

"Because we didn't get our Good Deed Merit Badges," said Sister.

"We couldn't find anyone to do a good deed *for*," said Brother.

"Well, it seems to me," said Mama, "that you *have* done a good deed. You got Papa home. And that is a very good deed, indeed."

"Your Mama's right," said
Papa. "I can feel it in my bones."
And he gave the Bear Scouts
their Good Deed Merit Badges
right then and there.